To Be Loved

humorous and heartwarming short stories

Very Large Print

Stefania Hartley

THE∗SICILIAN∗MAMA

ISBN: 978-1-914606-38-0

Stefania Hartley asserts the moral right to be identified as the author of this work.

This is a work of fiction. Names, characters and events are solely the product of the author's imagination.

These stories were first published in The People's Friend magazine.

Cover by Joseph Witchall

To Susanna x

CONTENTS

1. A PERFECT COMBINATION

Mark compared the mirror with the photo from his youth and found the mirror wanting, especially of hair. Unfortunately, the young man with the rock star's shock of hair was the one Nora remembered, not the bald, middle-aged gentleman he had turned into.

Then there was the missing leg. He still hadn't told her about the motorbike accident where he'd lost part of his left leg.

But the man in the mirror hadn't just lost things. He had also gained: extra buoyancy around the waist, a beginning of wings under the arms and an all-new jowl.

And now Mark regretted suggesting that they met in person, because it was going to take a miracle for his old sweetheart to recognise him. But, deep down, he believed in miracles.

***

Nora put on her biggest pair of sunglasses and looked at herself in the mirror.

They did a great job at hiding the wrinkles around her eyes, but she hoped it was a very sunny day or she'd be virtually blind. And there was still her neck. Her more famous namesake, Nora Ephron, had said that necks don't lie about a woman's age.

Nora pinched the loose skin under her chin. Not quite a wattle yet, but on the way. She rummaged in her accessories drawer and tried on different scarves. She settled on a red silk scarf, the colour so intense that it reflected a flattering pink blush on her cheeks.

Her next problem was her hair. The last time Mark had seen her it had been long, flowy and brown. Now it was a grey pixie cut.

She could colour it without difficulty, but making it longer was another matter. Hair extensions were too expensive and she worried about how ethically they might be sourced. Also, if she suddenly turned up at work with long hair, there would be endless questions from her colleagues. Her class of inquisitive six-year-olds would be especially curious.

She should have never agreed to this meeting. Without social media profiles, she and Mark had no idea what the other looked like, and it was probably best kept this way. Mark was going to be disappointed to find that the leather-clad rock chick he had dated was now a boring middle-aged primary school teacher.

What if he didn't recognise her when he saw her? Or recognised her but didn't like her?

The last few months, after a mutual friend had put them in touch again, had been the happiest months since her divorce. She had a feeling that this meeting was going to ruin everything. But it was too late to call it off, too late to grow her hair, too late to be the girl she had been.

Maybe there was something she could do about her hair. She picked up her wallet and rushed out of the house.

***

Yes, Mark believed in miracles, but not the kind hair clinics promised in their adverts. And certainly not for those amounts of money. Instead, he went to a hat shop.

The shop assistant—reassuringly also bald—was very helpful. He produced flat caps and fedora hats, trilbies and boaters, panamas and porkpies, but none of them pleased Mark.

"I'm looking for rockstar vibes," Mark confessed.

The shop assistant searched on his phone and showed Mark a photo of Angus Young in a green baseball cap, wearing what looked like a school uniform.

"Not that kind," Mark replied.

The man showed him a black-and-white photo of a young Mick Jagger defiantly donning a black top hat.

"Perhaps not that either."

Jimi Hendrix's hat looked a lot better, but the shop didn't stock it. Mark eventually settled for an Aussie sun hat that gave him a dangerous and adventurous look but fell short of turning him into a cowboy.

"It looks perfect, and it's very light too," the shop assistant commented.

Mark completed the outfit

with sturdy jeans that covered his prosthetic leg, a good-looking belt and a patterned shirt to wear with the cuffs casually rolled up. He didn't look exactly like his young self, but at least he looked like he had made an effort.

He hoped that would be good enough.

***

It was a breezy, sunny summer's day and the park was teeming with people.

Both Nora and Mark were half an hour early to the

appointment by the ice cream kiosk. At first Nora didn't recognise the man in the hat, but as soon as he smiled at her, her heart fluttered. Yes. There was the young man she had fallen in love with all those years ago.

She flicked her hair off her shoulders self-consciously and pushed her hat down on her head. They embraced awkwardly, then he told her that she hadn't changed much. She didn't believe his words, but then he had always been a sweet man.

How different her life would have been if she hadn't turned him down when he asked her to marry him. If only she'd been brave enough to leave her hometown and family to follow him to where his new job was taking him.

When they ordered their ice creams, Mark still remembered her favourite flavour.

"You haven't forgotten," Nora said.

"I haven't forgotten anything," he replied slowly.

"I'm sorry. I made mistakes," she admitted.

"We both did," he replied. "We were young. After two months, I was made redundant from that job. I should have never taken it."

"And I could have waited for you," she said. "Why did you never marry anyone else?"

"I never met the right woman—another one," he answered.

Her heart beat faster. Was it too late to correct their mistakes?

***

As soon as Mark had seen her, all the old feelings had rushed back.

He had never stopped loving her. Being near her made his heart soar.

But, just then, his hat soared on a gust of wind.

"Your hat!" Nora shouted, running after it.

But the wind snatched hers, too. They both chuckled as they helplessly watched their runaway hats spin round each other in an aerial dance. The wind deposited them on the branches of a nearby tree.

Now that the secret of his baldness was out, Mark would have happily left his hat there, but Nora was holding her head as if she missed hers.

"I'll get them," he offered.

The tree was in a private garden, but its branches hung over a low wall. If he climbed on it, he should be able to reach.

"Be careful," Nora said, which felt nice because it meant that she cared.

But the branch looked closer from the ground than it did once he was on the wall. He couldn't reach the hats without stepping onto the tree. Did it count as trespass if he got onto the tree without touching the ground?

Their hats weren't the only things the branches had trapped. Mark pulled out a Frisbee and threw it back into the park without looking. Then he got the hats and was about to throw them down too when, suddenly, something black and fast shot out of a corner of the garden, barking wildly.

***

Nora's heart jumped into her mouth. It would be the cruellest twist of fate that would take Mark from her just after they had been reunited!

"Watch out for the dog!" she warned him, but the Doberman leapt and got him by the ankle.

Nora screamed. People came out of the house shouting, but the dog wasn't letting go.

Nora was sure that Mark was in terrible pain, but he wasn't

making any sound.

Suddenly, there was a sound of ripping fabric. The dog staggered back with Mark's leg in its mouth! At that point, for Nora everything went black and she fainted.

***

Mark had never been happier to have a prosthetic leg.

The dog seemed as shocked as its owners, who apologised profusely. Mark reassured them that he had lost his leg—the real one—on another occasion, and apologised for the intrusion and the commotion he had caused.

Once the dog was safely locked indoors and all explanations and apologies had been exchanged, the leg was returned to Mark. Except for some small dents and dog saliva, it was still in good shape.

Not the same could be said about Mark's trousers. They looked like they had had an encounter with a ravenous shark.

Leg back on, Mark climbed

off the tree and slid off the wall. This wasn't the way he had planned for Nora to find out about his prosthetic limb. Mark scanned the lawn, searching for her.

And found her.

He took in her legs, stretched on the grass. There was a crowd surrounding her. Her hair was too far from her body. A streak of red on the grass...

He froze.

He should have looked before throwing that Frisbee. Instead, he had decapitated

her!

***

Through the feet of the crowd, Nora recognised Mark's shoes approaching. How could it be, if he'd just had his leg bitten off?

His head peeked through the crowd of people who had come to her aid. His face was ashen.

"Your leg?" she asked him.

"Miracles do happen," he said.

"A miracle on your leg?"

"No. On your neck."

Nora touched her neck.

Likely to help her breathe, someone had untied her scarf, which now lay on the grass.

Her neck was exposed. So was her real hair. The wig she had been wearing was lying on the grass near the scarf. She raised her sunglasses, too, and smiled at Mark. There was nothing left to hide now.

***

Once they were alone again, Mark showed Nora his prosthetic leg. She said that this made him an enhanced bionic man, which flattered him. They both agreed that he had been very lucky that the dog had chosen that leg instead of the other.

Then Nora showed him her wig and Mark said that he really liked her pixie cut. Nora only noticed Mark's baldness when he pointed it out, which made them both chuckle. And her neck was just lovely, Mark said, and he was very glad that it was still in one piece despite his careless Frisbee launch.

"I was really worried for you," Nora admitted.

"And I for you," he replied. "I'm sorry, but I think I'm still in love with you, Nora."

"Why are you sorry?" she asked with a look of concern.

"If I wasn't enough for you when we were young, how can I be enough for you now?" Mark asked. "So much of the old me is missing."

"I think it was me who missed something back then: courage," she said. "And now, what I'm missing is you."

She rocked on the balls of her feet and kissed him.

2. LOST AT SEA

Salvatore turned the tiller and headed home after a night's fishing. The rising sun glittered over the crispy waves of the Gulf of Catania, Sicily, and the engine rumbled soothingly.

He loved the sea. The fish were treasure, the birds were company and the water was solace. He needed solace.

The paint on the boat, where he had changed her name to *Rosaria*, had dried now, but his tears hadn't quite.

He still felt a lump in his throat every time he returned home to an empty house.

One day, returning from a fishing trip, he had found Rosaria waiting for him on her chair, beautifully smiling in a sleep from which she couldn't wake up. The doctor had said that her heart had given out.

A pair of seagulls sat on the roof of the cabin. He smiled at them and they seemed to nod a greeting back.

Seagulls paired for life, just like people. That was why he still wore his wedding ring, even if it slipped off his finger these days.

Before heading home, he had hauled in his nets, harvesting the commercially viable fish that were caught in them and throwing starfish, sea cucumber and pebbles back into the water.

An octopus had become entangled too. It would fetch a

good price at the fish market. Salvatore had started disentangling it, but the creature was working against him. Having more tentacles than a man has limbs, it had a stark advantage. Eventually, Salvatore had managed to put the octopus into a bucket.

When all the fish were in the boat and the nets were piled in a corner of the boat, Salvatore had turned on the engine and headed back home.

But as his gaze had fallen upon his hands on the wheel, a

strip of untanned skin had glared at him from the place where his wedding ring had always been. He cut the engine. He had lost his ring.

***

Salvatore had searched every bucket, every pile of nets, every nook and cranny of the boat, but there was no sign of his wedding ring anywhere. The sun was high in the sky when he gave up searching.

He peered over the side of the boat into the deep blue. His wedding ring must have joined all the other treasures that the sea hid in its depths.

Maybe this was a sign that it was time he stopped grieving: a sea burial for his grief.

"Goodbye," he said to the blue waters, then turned on the engine and let his boat chug back to the shore.

At the dock, he arranged his catch neatly in wooden crates over beds of ice and sold them to the wholesalers. That morning, his fish would be on fishmongers' stalls for people to buy.

He washed down his boat, cleaned his nets and repaired the holes, then went home.

***

Giovanna went to the market with her shopping trolley, even if she didn't need a trolley now that she only shopped for one.

The fishmonger and the greengrocer, from their stalls opposite each other, were shouting the praises of their wares at increasingly louder volumes. The fishmonger's more piercing tenor voice won Giovanna's attention. It would be nice to have fish for lunch.

Crates packed with ice and seaweed were stacked up on the road, waiting to take pride of place on the steel display tables. From the side, Giovanna noticed a pair of tentacles wrapped around the outside of one of the crates.

An octopus.

Ciro, her late husband, had loved octopus, and so did she. Maybe she could treat herself to some octopus today.

She touched his wedding ring, which she wore on top of

hers. It was loose on her finger, but her own tighter ring kept it secure. Ciro had been far from the perfect husband but she had loved him all the same.

"Do you have octopus in that crate? How much is it?" she asked the fishmonger.

"Yes, I have octopus. Thirty euros per kilo."

That sounded like a lot of money, but she must remember that she wouldn't need more than a few hundred grams.

"I'll have the smallest you've got."

"Sorry, you can't."

The fishmonger extracted the crate from the pile and Giovanna saw why she couldn't: it was just one big octopus.

The man whipped it onto the scale. "A bit over one kilo. I'll charge you only thirty euros because you've saved me the trouble to put it out and write a label. Okay?"

"No, no, no! It's way too big for me. Can I have less?"

"I don't sell octopuses by the tentacle," the man scoffed. "It's the whole or nothing."

She could have said no, but the octopus was already on the scale and the man was twisting the waterproof paper around his fist to make a packaging cone.

It felt offensive to the octopus and to the man to say no now. She would just have to share it with her neighbour, or cut it up and freeze it. "I'll take it."

She parted with her money

and took her magnificent treat home.

When she opened the parcel on the kitchen's draining board, the smell of the sea hit her nostrils. She loved the sea. She hadn't been to the seaside for a while. Maybe she should make a trip.

She admired the octopus. It was a beautiful creature, and perhaps too beautiful to eat. She'd better make this her last.

She turned it upside-down to prepare it for cooking, when

something shiny caught her eye. A gold ring? What was an octopus doing with a gold ring among its tentacles?

For a moment, Giovanna imagined a crown for a royal merbaby, a collar for a seahorse, a belt for a wealthy eel. She turned it in her hands. It was a human wedding ring, and the names of the giver and the recipient were engraved inside.

She didn't think about the bargain she had struck, getting gold at the price per kilo of an octopus. All she could think of was that a man had lost his wedding ring and was likely looking for it.

She had to reunite the ring with its owner.

***

Giovanna had to wait until the next morning, when the market was open again.

As soon as the fishmonger saw her, he smiled. "Was the octopus good?"

Giovanna checked the man's ring finger. He had a ring on, so he couldn't have been the one who had lost it.

"I found a wedding ring tucked under its tentacles," she replied.

"Then it must have been a married octopus!" the man joked.

Giovanna didn't smile. This was a serious matter. "Do you have any idea who the ring might belong to?"

"If you leave it with me, I'll ask at the fish market," the fishmonger offered.

What should she do? Giving the ring to the fishmonger and

letting him sort it out was the easiest thing. But a wedding ring wasn't just an object of emotional value—it was a piece of gold. Heaven forbid it ended up being sold off to a jeweller for money.

She couldn't risk it. Even if the prospect of venturing by herself into the wholesale fish market scared her, she would have to do it.

"If you tell me who you bought the octopus from, I'll go myself," she replied.

"As you wish. You'd better

hurry, because it closes at nine."

"Nine in the morning?"

"Yes. It opens at three a.m. and closes at nine a.m. We're up early so you can have fresh fish in the morning," he explained.

"Thank you. It's much appreciated."

After taking a number of buses, Giovanna reached the wholesale fish market.

Some sellers had already closed for the day but, thankfully, the man she was looking for was still there.

"I'm not married," the man told her.

"Have you any idea who could have lost a wedding ring?"

"Unless it belongs to one of the fishermen I buy from, I have no idea."

Giovanna thought for a moment. "Can you remember buying a big octopus yesterday?"

"Oh, yes. A beautiful octopus," the man replied.

"Do you know the name of

the fisherman you bought it from?"

"Yes, he's a great chap. We all like him. His name is Totò."

Totò was a common nickname for Salvatore, the name engraved in the ring. She had found the owner.

***

Salvatore was getting the boat ready for another night's fishing. He'd always liked going out fishing, but he liked it even more now that the sea held his wedding ring.

At the docks, the other

fishermen were setting up their boats too. Everyone was on their own but, in a way, they were together, joined by the indivisible waters of the sea.

A figure that didn't look like a fisherman came down the wharf with the gait of someone who had business to accomplish.

A woman. Maybe a wife or a sister of one of the other fishermen, bringing him a packed breakfast that he had forgotten at home. A little pang of envy stabbed at him.

The woman spoke to the first fisherman. He shook his head and she moved on to the next boat. Maybe she was a customer, trying to buy fish before the boats set off? She must realise that the sea didn't accept pre-orders.

When she reached him, he was ready to explain that the sea gave what it gave, and often took instead.

"Do you happen to know anybody who has lost a wedding ring?" she asked instead.

Surprise, confusion and hope swirled in his brain. "How do you know?"

She smiled at him. She had a beautiful smile. "Because I've found it."

"But I lost it in the sea," Salvatore argued.

"It seems that an octopus found it for you."

Salvatore remembered the octopus that had wrestled him.

"I bought the octopus," she added, then glanced at the boat where he had painted

Rosaria's name. "Due diligence would require me asking your name and your wife's name to see if they match the engraving, but seeing as you've named your boat *Rosaria*, all I need is confirmation that you are Salvatore."

Salvatore nodded. "Thank you," he said once he had recovered the power of speech.

"Some things are important."

She showed him her hand with two wedding rings, one

bigger and one smaller, and he understood. Better, he'd found someone who understood him.

"How can I thank you?" he asked.

She looked at the sun setting behind the sea, and hesitated. "I love the sea. Maybe you could let me come fishing with you sometime? I'll help as much as I can."

"It will be my pleasure," he replied, beckoning her onto the deck.

"Now?"

"Yes, why not?"

Their smiles met.

That night, Salvatore and Giovanna caught many fish and another octopus, but they returned the octopus to the sea.

"Octopuses have three hearts. It's a shame that we humans have only one," Salvatore remarked.

"Yes, but ours is big enough to hold many people," Giovanna replied.

It was the first of many fishing trips together, and they never took an octopus out of

the sea again.

3. A WARM WELCOME

The warmth of love was all very good, but there were times when Melina needed some real warmth too.

Even in Palermo, wintertime was often cold and wet, and today it was also windy.

The windowpanes of the sitting room rattled and whistled, and a chilly draught blew under the doors and bit Melina's ankles.

"What time does the heating come on?" she asked her husband, even though she knew the answer.

Tanino lifted his gaze from the crossword. He was wrapped in two plaid blankets, with only his hands sticking out. Bello, their dog, poked his head out of the plaids.

"Sorry, I can't turn the heating on. It's too windy," Tanino answered.

Melina bristled. "It's absurd

that we can't have the heating on when we need it most."

"The wind blows out the flame of the boiler," Tanino said.

"It's okay for you—you can stay wrapped up in your chair—but I have to be up and about in the kitchen."

"You could warm yourself up with the oven?" he suggested sheepishly.

She shot him a look that she hoped was icier than the draughts swirling around her feet.

"Okay, I'll see if I can turn the heating on."

He emerged from his blankets and went out onto the balcony.

Melina watched anxiously from behind the glass of the French door as Tanino pressed the ignition button over and over. The flame came on and immediately died. He came back inside, shaking his head.

"I've tried. It's not possible," he said, then went to the hall, shrugged into his coat, and left.

Melina was incensed. How could he have the heart to leave her shivering at home all alone? He must be going to his usual café, to weather it out in the steamy warmth. Melina felt her blood boil, but even that didn't warm her up enough. So she called her sister-in-law and explained the situation.

"There's only one solution, darling," Fina said.

***

"We can't install a new boiler until next week. All our men are busy," the shopkeeper told

Tanino.

"But I can't wait! My wife is shivering at home," Tanino said.

"Then buy one of our oil heaters," the man suggested, showing Tanino round the shop.

"I'll have this one," Tanino said, pointing to the cheapest heater on display. It was as small as his dog.

"If you have heating problems, you need something bigger," the man said, patting a heater as big as a Great

Dane. The price tag matched the size.

"Have you got anything else?" Tanino asked.

"Nothing that will do the job you're after."

Tanino sighed. "Okay...I'll buy this one," he said, opening his wallet.

But as soon as the man handed him the box with the heater, Tanino realised that he had a problem.

He had come on foot and the box wasn't just bulky, but heavy too. "Do you do home deliveries?"

"Yes. The next available slot is next Thursday."

"But that's after you come and fit my boiler!"

The man shrugged.

"I'll have to go home and get the car," Tanino said.

"We're closing in fifteen minutes."

He could never make it. His brother, Ciccio, lived just around the corner and he wouldn't mind coming to his rescue, but... Tanino would have to explain to him why he needed a heater so urgently, and Ciccio would berate him for not fixing the boiler's issue before. Tanino had meant to replace it ages ago, but he only thought about it when the weather was windy.

But if he wanted the heater in his flat tonight, he had no choice but to ask his brother for help. Tanino swallowed his pride and rang Ciccio.

***

"Let me understand: you can't turn the heating on when it's windy?" his brother asked as soon as they were alone in the car.

"Yes. The boiler is on the kitchen balcony, and when it's windy the flame is blown out."

"So you haven't got any heating at the moment?"

"No. I've bought a new boiler but they won't install it until next week." Tanino noticed that they were on the wrong road. "This isn't the way to my flat."

"We're not going to your flat. We're going to mine," Ciccio said with a smile.

"I've got to go home. Melina is waiting for me."

Ciccio patted his arm. "Or maybe she's not."

***

As soon as Fina opened the door, Melina felt warm air tumble out of the flat. Fina pulled her into the flat with a hug while, on Melina's lead, Bello barked, wagging his tail.

"Oh, beautiful boy, I've missed you!" Fina said, crouching to stroke him.

When Tanino had first come home with Bello, Fina and

Ciccio had kept him in their flat until Melina had conquered her fear of dogs and had fallen in love with Bello. Now the dog lived with Melina and Tanino.

Fina invited Melina to sit on the sofa, offered her a cup of coffee and gave her a pair of warm slippers.

Fina gave Bello a biscuit and they all sat on the sofa together. Melina was pleasantly thawing, and it wasn't just because the flat was toasty. It was Fina's affection.

This was a warm welcome in every way. What a far cry from her callous husband, leaving her shivering at home while he went to the café!

"Where is Ciccio?" she asked her sister-in-law.

Fina smiled. "He's gone to rescue Tanino."

"From what?"

"Hasn't he told you? He went to the shops and bought an oil heater but couldn't carry it home on foot, so he asked Ciccio to pick him up in the car.

So Tanino hadn't gone to the

café with his friends! The last bit of Melina to thaw now was her heart.

A moment later, the door opened and the brothers walked in with a large box. They didn't even take their coats off before they pulled the oil heater out of its box and plugged it into the wall to check if it worked.

"Thank you very much, Ciccio. Would you mind driving us all home with the heater?" Tanino asked his brother.

"I'm only driving you home if

it's to pack your overnight bags: you're staying with us until your boiler is sorted or the wind dies down," Ciccio said.

Fina clapped her hands. "What a good idea. Please, say yes!"

There was nothing Melina wanted more than to spend a few days with her sister-in-law, and judging by the fact that Bello was rolling on his back, he didn't have any objections either.

Tanino exchanged a glance

with Melina, then answered his brother. "That's very kind. Thank you."

"Don't thank me. I'm putting up with you only because we like Bello!" Ciccio said with a good-humoured chuckle.

Tanino, too, received a pair of warmed slippers and they all shared a hot dinner, then watched TV together with Bello stretched between them.

The warmth of Fina and Ciccio's central heating was lovely, but what was really special was the warmth of family. And right now, Melina was having it all.

4. WRITTEN IN THE STARS

Since the new sub editor had joined the magazine, Arianna had been going to work with a bounce in her step.

Her job as features writer hadn't changed, but now that Luigi read every one of her articles, even if only to check them for errors, she made a special effort.

She'd also put extra effort into her appearance since Luigi had started, and some of her female colleagues had noticed.

But had Luigi? If she didn't count the time she spent writing articles and the time he took to proofread them, they hadn't been in each other's company much. Occasionally, they travelled together in the lift, but there was no conversation. Too awkward.

Once, he'd emailed her to praise her feature on birds that

paired for life. For weeks afterwards she'd wondered if it had been a coded love message.

In response, on his birthday, when he brought in a homemade hazelnut and chocolate gianduja cake, she told him that she liked men who baked. He'd blushed as red as his birthday tie. It had to be a sign that he was interested in her too.

But the next step—meeting outside the office—was too scary.

What if she asked him out and he wasn't interested? Working together would be awkward afterwards. She'd do better carrying on writing articles about birds pairing for life and waiting for him to make the first move.

***

When Monia, the editor-in-chief, asked to see her, Arianna feared the worst.

A meeting with the boss could only be one of two things: good news or bad news. Had Monia found out that she was infatuated with a colleague?

Monia welcomed her with a smile. "I like your latest articles. You've really upped your game."

Arianna beamed.

"I'd like you to write our new horoscope page."

Arianna coughed with surprise. "I'm not an astrologer."

"That's not an issue. All you need to do is come up with a few lines of common sense and advice."

Even if she didn't believe in horoscopes, Arianna was sure that it was more than that. But in three years at the magazine, she'd learnt there was no point arguing with Monia, so she said yes, went back to her desk and started writing.

***

One week later, Arianna found Luigi lingering at the water cooler.

"Congratulations on your Starstruck Horoscope. I didn't know Sophia Lauren is a Virgo and Lauren isn't her real name," Luigi told her.

The celebrity angle and the "Starstruck" title had been Arianna's idea—the one thing she was proud of. "You've read my horoscopes column?"

"I proofread it. I don't usually read horoscopes, but yours was spot on."

"Thank you."

There was a reason why his horoscope was spot on. Arianna had remembered which day he'd brought in the birthday cake, and working out that he was a Taurus, had taken inspiration to write her horoscope for Taurus.

Your diligence and attention to detail are serving you well in your new job. Your colleagues appreciate you...

She'd had no idea he had been assigned to proofread the horoscopes too.

***

Arianna read the Taurus horoscope one last time.

It's a time of new beginnings. If there's anything you've wanted to do but haven't been brave enough, now is the time to take the plunge.

She clicked Send and leaned back in her chair. Hopefully, if Luigi was interested in her like she was in him, his horoscope would prompt him to ask her out.

A few days later, as she met him in the lift lobby, he welcomed her with a smile.

"Your horoscope has given me the push I needed to sell my car. I don't need it now I live in the city, but I was afraid to let go. Thank you."

Arianna smiled. Selling his car wasn't the brave step she had hoped he'd make, but if it earned her brownie points with him, she was probably going in the right direction.

Maybe she needed to be more explicit.

***

This is a good week to cultivate relationships in the workplace, read the next horoscope for Taurus.

At the start of the week, Arianna ventured into Luigi's side of the office and walked by his desk.

"Hello, Luigi. Have you ever had lunch at the café downstairs? They make excellent pasta and pizza," she suggested hopefully.

"That's good to know. I'm about to go there with the guys from the post room."

"That's... great," she said, forcing a smile.

"Fancy coming too?"

"Thanks, but I'm busy."

She didn't know the guys from the post room, and going together wouldn't exactly be a date. Clearly, Luigi had misunderstood his horoscope. She had better be clearer next week.

She carefully wrote the following week's horoscope for Taurus.

The stars are aligned for you in the love department. If there's a special someone you'd like to ask out, this is a good time to make that first step.

She couldn't have been more explicit. Now all she could do was sit back and wait.

***

A few days had passed and Arianna hadn't bumped into Luigi. Was he hiding from her? Had she pushed her luck with her last horoscope?

Eventually, she ambled over to his desk. It was empty. A horrible realisation dawned on her. He must have taken time off to act on her advice... with someone else!

Pictures of Luigi lying on a beach with someone else popped into her mind. What a disaster!

***

Luigi tossed and turned in his bed. His head throbbed and his nose ran. He hated having a cold, but this time he was also annoyed about being stuck at home.

He liked going to work, reading his colleagues' pieces, meeting them by the lift, chatting with them by the water cooler. If he were honest, he missed Arianna. Crikey, was he falling in love?

There was only one way to find out: by asking her out. But

he wasn't brave enough for that. What if she turned him down? He'd better be content with reading her work.

As he hadn't proofread that week's issue, he picked up a copy of the magazine from his bedside table and flicked to Arianna's articles.

That week, she'd written a feature about aphrodisiac plants, an insert about engagement rituals in different cultures, and the usual horoscope.

As he read it, his jaw

dropped. The stars of love were aligned for him this week! He must get back to the office before the week was over!

**

Arianna tried to concentrate on her article about baking techniques around the world, but all she could think of was her favourite baker on a romantic holiday with someone else. Perhaps a stroll to the water cooler would clear her mind.

Since she'd found out that

Luigi was off and she'd had no more hopes of meeting him, she had hardly left her desk. She was getting up from her chair when Luigi appeared at her desk.

"Hello." Instead of tanned and refreshed, he looked pale and peaky. He smiled broadly.

"How was your holiday?"

"Holiday?" He chuckled. "I've been off sick."

"I'm sorry," she replied, trying to suppress a huge smile.

"I'm better now. Would you

like to have lunch with me later?" he asked.

"You want to have lunch with me?"

Even before his words, the pink blush on his pale cheeks confirmed that he had asked her for a date. "Yes, I do."

Arianna's chest tingled with excitement. She already had an idea for next week's horoscope. *A recent surprise encounter could lead to everlasting happiness.*

5. TO BE LOVED

Amanda knew that her name meant "she who must be loved". But instead of taking it for what it was—a parents' hopeful wish—she took it as a duty to make herself lovable.

She had become so skilled at moulding herself to the expectations of the people around her that she often forgot her real self.

It was hard work making herself likeable, especially when other people's expectations weren't obvious to her. Like at this dentistry conference in Rome.

In England, Amanda knew the expectations, but she was out of her depth here. Was she supposed to queue for the taxi or mill around like the others? Was tipping the waiter in the restaurant offensive or required? The saying "When in Rome, do as the Romans" was very good so long as you knew what the Romans did.

In her hotel room, she slipped into her evening gown, applied the last stroke of mascara and checked in the mirror. She looked perfect for the conference's opening dinner.

***

When her taxi deposited her at the venue, she couldn't believe her eyes. While she was wrapped in layers of chiffon, all the other attendees were wearing semi-formal work clothes.

Wasn't Italy the home of Valentino, Versace and Prada? A quick dash back to the hotel was urgently required. She was about to hail another taxi when someone called her.

"Hello, Amanda."

She turned around. It was a man with the warmest, most handsome eyes she had ever seen.

"Hello. Do we know each other?"

"I read your name on your badge," he said with an Italian

accent. He pointed to the name badge she had pinned to her handbag. "I'm Riccardo," he added, offering his hand. "Are you on your own?"

"Yes."

"So am I. Shall we go in together? I always find it a bit intimidating walking into a room full of people."

His suggestion was very appealing but the urge to change her dress and conform was too strong.

"Actually, I was just about to nip back to the hotel and get changed," she admitted.

He looked surprised. "Why?"

"It looks like I'm not following the dress code," she explained.

"Do you like your dress?"

"Er, yes." She would have liked to ask him if he liked it too, but realized that it would be inappropriate.

"Is it comfortable?"

Amanda smiled. It seemed very Italian to consider the beauty of the dress before its comfort.

"It's very comfortable."

"Then there's no reason why you should change it," he said simply.

He took her hand and wrapped it around the crook of his elbow. "May I take you inside?"

She glanced at the other women around her in black trousers and blouses, then at her gown of pink chiffon and made a decision. "Yes, please."

As they strode elegantly into the dining hall, she didn't feel out of place. She felt like a princess.

As they chatted with each other and the other people at their table, Amanda liked Riccardo more and more. For the first time in her life, she didn't feel like she needed to earn approval. She'd felt his approval from the moment they'd met.

***

That evening, Amanda was sad to say goodnight.

"See you for breakfast?" Riccardo asked.

She nodded eagerly.

"I'll be waiting for you," he

said, but she wasn't sure if he meant it.

Sleep didn't grace her bed that night. She replayed all their conversations in her head and insecurity struck her.

Maybe he didn't like her as much as she liked him, and had kept her company out of politeness.

But the next morning, when she entered the hotel's breakfast hall, a hand waved at her from a little table for two.

Riccardo! Her heart floated in

her chest.

"Morning, Amanda. Have you slept well?"

"I have. How about you?"

She wasn't going to tell him that she had spent the night thinking about him instead of sleeping.

"Not really," Riccardo admitted.

Was it rude to ask why or not to ask it? After a little hesitation, she went with her heart. "Why?"

"I was thinking of you."

"Pardon?" Had he really said

that?

"I'm sorry, I'm being too sincere. It's a problem I have."

Amanda's heart flipped inside her chest.

"I don't see it as a problem," she replied. "Your sincerity, I mean. And thinking of me...that's quite all right too."

"But I'm always sincere about everything, good and bad. That's my problem."

Amanda grinned. "That's wonderful. You can't imagine how liberating it is to know that!"

He gave her a puzzled look.

"I wouldn't have to worry about getting on other people's nerves if I knew that they'd tell me," she explained.

Riccardo smiled. "I can assure you that you're not getting on my nerves but, rather, on my *cuore*."

After breakfast, Amanda hid in the toilet and used her phone to search what *cuore* meant. It meant "heart".

***

The last day of the conference was a sad time.

After saying goodbye to their fellow attendees, Riccardo suggested that he take her on a tour of Rome on his Vespa.

She agreed, even though she wasn't sure about mopeds and Italian roads. But her fears disappeared when they set off.

As they strolled along the Foro Romano, he turned to her. "Do you know your name comes from Latin? It means 'She who must be loved'."

"Yes, I do," she said with a sigh.

"Why do you sound so down

about it?" he asked.

"Because it's hard work to make sure it comes true."

He shook his head. "That's not your job to do, Amanda." He held her hand and smiled. "From now on, it's mine."

6. ALWAYS A BEAUTY

After a day like that, Beth needed a refreshing drink. She perched herself on one of the empty barstools and ordered a martini.

She had returned to her hometown to help her sister organise her wedding but, instead of ringing photographers and catering companies, that morning they had rung for the paramedics.

There was no messing around with asthma attacks. Thankfully, they had arrived quickly and her sister was out of danger, but Beth was still a little shaken.

An old Jennifer Lopez song played in the background—the same song that had been playing the night she turned eighteen.

In a cloud of perfume, hair spray and face glitter, she had waltzed in with her friends and their feather boas, demanding drinks. The barman—her neighbour and childhood friend—hadn't had to ID her because he knew full well that it was her birthday.

"It's still two hours to the time you were born, so I can't serve you yet...unless you bribe me with a kiss," he'd teased.

To the sound of whooping and cheering, she'd walked round the bar and aimed a kiss at his cheek, but he'd turned at the last minute and her kiss had landed on his lips. The other girls swore it was obvious that he liked her, but she brushed them off. Handsome guys like him didn't date girls like her.

The new barman tonight was a young guy she had never seen before. She brought her glass to her lips, but it was empty.

"May I get you another one?" a male voice asked her.

Beth turned and almost dropped her glass. A sandy-haired blue-eyed man sat on the stool next to her. And she knew him.

She hadn't seen him for ten years. The sharp jaw and the broad shoulders were new, but Mike Robinson still looked every bit like the school's heartthrob. And he still took her breath away.

Her heart rattled the bars of her ribcage just like it had every time he had walked past her in the school corridors. The confident, grown-up woman instantly reverted to the insecure teenager.

"Hi," she said quietly.

She urged herself to get a grip. She had lost all her extra pounds since school, but a lifetime's insecurity habit was hard to break.

"I'm Mike," he said with a warm smile.

Beth's heart froze. He didn't remember her. They'd shared English, Maths and Science classes, they had sat in the same row, and once or twice they had been paired for groupwork. But he didn't remember her.

The words of a large woman who had once been interviewed on TV came back to her mind. "The bigger you are, the more invisible," the woman had said. The proof was before her eyes.

"I'm Beth Sanderson."

His face fell. Oh, dear. His reaction could only mean one thing—he had just remembered her and it wasn't a good memory. The stigma of her past was still on her.

Beth started to count how long it would take him to make

excuses and leave. But he didn't.

He flashed her a killer smile and offered his hand. "Mike Robinson."

Phew. He hadn't recognised her after all. At first she had been offended by his lack of recognition, and now she was relieved about it. Although it felt weird, she shook his hand as if they were strangers meeting for the first time.

"Another martini?" he asked.

"Yes, please."

It saddened her that he had

never noticed her when she was overweight, despite being in class together, but now that she was slim he was chatting her up in a pub. But the glow of his attention was warm and soft, and she enjoyed basking in it too much to leave.

"So what do you do?" he asked.

"I work for a solicitor's firm in London, but I grew up here," she answered. "I'm visiting my sister at the moment."

"Of course you are."

He took a gulp from his glass, then gave her a strange smile that left her puzzled. Was he teasing her about something?

"And what do you do?" she asked.

He shook his head slowly and clicked his tongue.

"You really don't remember me, do you, Beth?"

What? "Excuse me, you're the one who doesn't remember me!" she protested.

He cocked an eyebrow and a smile kicked up at the corner

of his lips.

"How's your sister feeling now?" he asked.

Beth brought both her hands to her cheeks. He was one of the paramedics who had rushed to help her sister that morning!

Now she remembered that he had said hello more warmly than a stranger would, but in her panic and fluster it hadn't clicked.

"I had finished my shift when your call came in, but I recognised the address and I volunteered to take your call," he said, looking shyly into his glass.

Beth's heart revved up again.

"What do you mean that you recognised the address?" she asked.

Her sister lived in what had been their parents' home, but Mike Robinson had had no reason to know where she lived as a teen.

He scratched the scruff of his neck.

"I had a bit of a crush on you when we were at school..." he revealed.

It was a good thing that he was a paramedic, because Beth felt like her heart might squeeze through her ribs and fly away. Mike, the guy she had fancied all through her school times, didn't just like her now that she was slim, but had liked her all along. The glass of martini slipped through her hands and landed on the bar, splashing Mike's shirt and trousers.

"I'm so sorry!" she exclaimed, jumping to grab a

handful of paper napkins to dry him, but stopping short of patting him dry.

"I'll get you another drink," he said, standing up and raising his hand to call the barman.

If someone had told her that Mike had an interest in her, she wouldn't have believed it— just like she hadn't believed that the former barman had liked her.

"Don't worry about my clothes," he told her. "I live just round the corner. I can go and get changed." He looked shyly at the floor. "Why don't you come over for a coffee?"

"Sure."

He offered her his arm and she took it. As they walked to his flat, arm in arm under a clear starry sky, Beth imagined herself interviewed on TV like that large woman she'd seen.

She would give her own pearl of wisdom: you were always a beauty.

7. FOR A WHITE WEDDING

The rain lashed at the 17th-century windows of Villa Lingualarga. Don Pericle looked hard at the couple sitting on the other side of the desk in his study.

By the second meeting, he had usually formed a good idea about the bride and groom who hoped to get married in his villa. He took care to find out why they wanted to be married, and if they should.

With Claudio and Mariella, he had a feeling that something was wrong, even if he couldn't put his finger on it.

They seemed very much in love, but there was an aura of resignation around them that didn't sit well with an engaged couple. It felt as if the wedding wasn't entirely welcome.

Asking indirect questions hadn't brought him closer to finding out what was wrong.

If, by the time their meeting was over, he hadn't reassured himself that all was well, he'd have to ask them openly whether they were sure about getting married or not.

Hopefully they'd give him a sincere answer, because he wouldn't let them marry at Villa Lingualarga if he wasn't convinced that they should.

"About the wines, these are my suggestions," he said, offering them a list he had scribbled with names of the best local wines.

The bride pushed it gently towards the groom. "You'd better choose, as I'm not having any," she said, stroking her tummy.

The bride was pregnant! Everything made sense now in Pericle's mind, and alarm bells clanged furiously.

If either of them had been pressured into marriage because there was a baby on the way, he must stop the wedding! First, he had to have a heart-to-heart with the bride and groom, each one on their own.

Pericle offered the couple drinks and took them on a long and unnecessary tour of the villa to prolong their stay until one of them needed the bathroom.

"You wouldn't be doing Mariella any favours if you married her out of duty," Pericle told the groom as soon as the bride had gone to the ladies'. "Both you and Mariella deserve a love marriage, even if it's not with each other," Pericle continued seriously.

Claudio chuckled. "Don Pericle, you really think that we're getting married only because Mariella is expecting a baby?"

"Well... the situation lends itself to the question."

A cloud came over Claudio's face. "That's exactly what I feared: getting married so quickly, everyone will think that we're doing it because of the baby. I told my parents and Mariella's parents, but they won't have it. I don't care so much about what other people think, but if our child grew up feeling responsible for our marriage, I would hate it. Mariella and I will surely have arguments in the future—it's normal—and I don't want our child to feel responsible about us. I love Mariella and I want to spend the rest of my life with her. I want us to be husband and wife. I just don't want anyone to think that the baby is the reason we're getting married."

Pericle sighed with relief. The situation wasn't as bad as

he had imagined. Now it was time to speak to the bride.

It was almost lunchtime when Pericle eventually managed to be alone with the bride. It had taken a tour of the villa, a perfunctory inspection of the crockery and cutlery and an impromptu visit to the cellar with wine sampling to get Claudio to go the bathroom.

Pericle sent him to the furthest one, deep in his private wing, so that he could be alone with the bride for long enough to ask the important question.

"If you weren't expecting his baby, would you still marry Claudio?"

Mariella shook her head decidedly. "Not at all. I love Claudio. Just..."

Oh, no, there was a but.

"Just not quite yet," she continued.

"Babies are born out of wedlock all the time," Pericle said. "If you don't feel ready for it, or are not sure, you shouldn't get married."

She chuckled. "I feel totally ready. I just don't like winter weddings. I've always dreamed of a spring wedding with birdsong, flowers and butterflies. But our parents would like us to get married before the bump becomes obvious. We want to make them happy. A wedding is still a wedding, and my dream of a spring wedding is just a whim. I shouldn't feel sad about missing out on it."

Mariella wanted spring, birdsong and flowers, and

Pericle wished he could provide them, but he couldn't. Not now.

"I'm sorry you aren't having the wedding of your dreams. I can't hasten spring, but I will do my best to make your wedding beautiful. A winter wedding doesn't have to be grey," Pericle said, and they both looked out the window at the garden hammered by the rain.

***

Claudio and Mariella had left hours ago, but the rain was

still pouring on Villa Lingualarga.

The evergreens were battered and droopy; bare trees and shrubs looked like sorry skeletons. What could he do to make the garden more cheerful on the day of the wedding?

When the rain finally eased, Pericle set off on a walk. It always helped him come up with solutions.

But not this time. He had walked into the town and still hadn't come up with any idea.

By now it was dark and the shopwindows glittered like jewels, especially the window of Angela's gift shop.

Pericle stopped to admire it. A bright patchwork elephant plush toy, a statuette of a shepherdess on a flowery bluff, a set of coloured candles decorated with pressed flowers, ceramic frogs leaping over each other... Everything on display was a splash of colour and life. An oasis of spring in the middle of winter. If Angela had managed to achieve it in her shop, maybe she could help him recreate spring in Villa Lingualarga's garden.

He walked in, greeted her and explained his problem.

"I have got just what you need," she said, disappearing into the back of the shop.

She returned with a large cardboard box and an excited smile. "They've only just arrived and I haven't had time to put them out yet, so you're the first customer to see them."

Angela opened the box and Pericle took a step back. It was a large swarm of butterflies, but none of them moved.

"They're paper butterflies," she explained. "Decorations."

Pericle chuckled and picked one up. Close up, it was clear it wasn't real, but from a distance it would look just like the real deal.

"I'll give you a discount for the whole box. I have flowers and origami birds too."

The birds were too angular to seem real, but they'd give a

touch of colour to the sombre green of the pines and cypresses. The flowers were perfect.

"I'll take the lot!"

"There's only one problem," Angela warned him. "They're made of paper so won't last long if it rains on them."

"If it rains on the day of the wedding, they'll be the least of my problems."

Pericle was sure that Mariella wouldn't appreciate a thunderstorm on her wedding. Unfortunately, the weather was something he couldn't control. All he could do was buy the spring props and ask friends and family to help him put them in the garden as close to the wedding as possible.

***

Early on that chilly winter morning, Pericle and his helpers got to work scattering the decorations around the garden: birds on trees, flowers in the flowerbeds and butterflies everywhere.

Pericle hadn't told Mariella

and Claudio about his plan. It would be a surprise, and he looked forward to seeing their faces.

They'd just finished setting up, and Pericle was feeling very pleased, when the sky clouded over.

As the pale winter sun disappeared behind a dark blanket, Pericle's happiness also drained away.

"It wasn't supposed to rain," he said to Angela, who had come to help.

"A cloud doesn't mean rain,"

she said.

But this wasn't just a cloud. It was a whole skyful of menacing lead. Even if those clouds held back their rain, they would obscure the sun. Under that drab grey light, all the paper flowers in the world could never make the garden look spring-like and cheerful.

If Mariella and Claudio's wedding wasn't a washout, it would be a gloomy day, and there was nothing he could do about it.

He had been foolish to think

he could fight nature's seasons and win.

***

The bride emerged from the car in a cloud of white tulle and faux fur.

She looked happy, but as soon as she gazed up to the ominous sky, the smile drained from her face. She rubbed her nose, then stared at the back of her hand. Something even whiter than her satin glove had landed on it.

From where he stood, under the archway of the door,

Pericle couldn't see exactly what it was, but it looked like dandelion fluff.

Mariella seemed just as puzzled and looked in Don Pericle's direction, as if the white substance might be something that he had organised.

He shrugged. More of the white fluff fell from the sky and landed on the bride and the groom, on the shiny car and the guests.

"Snow!"

"It's snowing!" everyone

cried.

Mariella's face broke into a smile. "Snow for confetti! Don Pericle, how did you do it?" she cried when she reached him.

Pericle smiled. "I'd love to be able to take the credit for this."

Even if they had been in Norway instead of Sicily, a fresh snowfall wouldn't have been guaranteed.

It was cold enough for the snow not to melt and the paper flowers, birds and butterflies remained crispy as new. The white background made them show up even more, and Mariella loved them.

"Don Pericle, a snowy wedding was beyond my wildest dreams! And I bet that no one has ever had a winter and a spring wedding all at once like this!"

Pericle kissed the bride's hand. "I wish you a life full of happy surprises beyond your wildest dreams."

Just then, he overheard someone talk to the groom. "I

hear that there's a baby on the way. Is this why you've rushed to get married?"

Claudio chuckled. "Not at all. We've rushed to catch the snow. Who hasn't dreamt of a white winter wedding?"

8. WE GO TOGETHER

Commotion and turmoil exploded in the Silicon Valley HQ of LoveDove, the creators of the world's biggest online dating app.

Doors were slammed, voices raised and coffee consumed by the gallon. The company's PR people worked their socks off and the programmers wore their fingers down to try to fix the software bug.

The famous infallible algorithm that had been matching lonely hearts the world over had suddenly gone rogue.

Nobody knew how it had happened. Conspiracy theories abounded. But the facts remained: millions of people all over the world were currently being matched regardless of their preferences, completely at random.

"Heads are going to roll if this isn't fixed immediately!" the boss told the staff.

It was taken as read that nobody would leave the office until the software bug was fixed.

Zak filled his mug with coffee and sat at his desk.

"Think of the hundreds of thousands of people who are being matched wrongly every minute," the boss told them.

But Zak couldn't feel sorry for them. At least they had time to look for a soulmate. He didn't even have that.

***

Antonio loved the Sicilian Spring. It wasn't hot like summer, and the air was full of birdsong, possibilities and promise.

He was about to step out of his flat to walk to the market when his phone tinkled in his pocket. It wasn't the same sound as text messages or missed calls. What could it be?

He took his phone out of his pocket and checked. A notification from the dating app he had signed up to months ago. In all that time, he'd never matched with anyone, so had forgotten all about it.

After years of attempts to find his soulmate, he had given up on real-life encounters and decided to try online dating.

Everyone around him seemed to have found love through it.

In real life, women always told him that he was nice, but there was always a reason why they wanted to remain just friends. Online dating was worse.

This notification had to be a reminder to renew his subscription or something equally boring. He tapped to open it and his eyebrows shot up. He had a match!

The phone almost slipped out of Antonio's hands as he scrolled her profile. She wasn't exactly his type, but the app must have matched them for a reason.

A message popped up. *Ciao, I'm Carolina. It seems that we've been matched.*

What should he reply? *Ciao. Yes, it seems so*, he typed. Safe enough. He added a smiley face for good measure, waited a full five seconds not to seem too keen, and sent it.

Three hours later, the two of them had had a long and witty conversation and had agreed to meet for lunch the next day.

By the time Antonio put his phone back in his pocket, the market was long shut but he didn't care. Now he was headed for the barbershop... and then to buy a new suit.

***

Carolina hadn't been too sure about this match. The guy's photo hadn't caught her interest, but he sounded witty and charming during their online chat, and if the dating app had recommended him there must be a reason.

Carolina had suggested meeting for lunch but the date didn't start too well.

As soon as she walked into the restaurant and he averted his gaze, she realized that he was shy. When he reached to greet her and knocked his glass of red wine over the table, he looked mortified.

Carolina felt like leaving just to put him out of his misery.

After the first painful attempts at conversation, she had an idea. "Do you know how to fold napkins into different shapes?"

"No. Do you?" he asked.

"I do it all the time in my job," she said, folding her napkin into a swan.

"Teach me."

By the time the first course arrived, they had made peacocks and hats, and had brushed fingers a few times in the process. The ice was broken.

Antonio turned out to be a very good listener, which suited Carolina very well. He was kind and polite to the waiters, which was very important to her. But how had the app known it? She had never ticked a box about that.

When the tiramisu arrived, Carolina thought that she had absolutely no need for a dessert called "pick-me-up".

The only thing she might need cheering up about was that their date was almost over.

"I have to confess that I was surprised when the dating app matched us," Carolina said, sinking her spoon into the mascarpone.

"This is the sweetest way a woman has ever told me that I'm not her type," Antonio replied.

"Oh, no. The app knew better," she hurried to explain.

"I've enjoyed this meal very much, and I hope to repeat it."

"Repeat it?" His eyebrows shot up.

"Yes. I'd like to see you again, if that's also your wish, of course."

Antonio's cheeks turned the colour of the wine left in his glass. He opened his mouth and closed it again without making a sound.

"I've put you on the spot, haven't I?" Carolina asked.

"You don't have to give me an answer—"

"I do! I do want to see you again!" Antonio exclaimed.

Now the crimson colour had crept up to his hairline. Carolina decided that it was time to ask for the bill.

***

Zak shut down his desktop computer. It had taken him and his team twenty-two hours to find the bug, but now the algorithm was fixed.

Finally they could go home for a shower, dinner, then bed.

While he slept, millions of app users were matched again according to their requirements. People around the world could find love again.

Zak traipsed to the elevator's lobby and pressed the button.

"Hey, Zak." It was Paige, one of the interface programmers.

He didn't much like her beanie hats and purple plaits, but she was nice. They rarely met because of their different shifts.

"Hey. Were you here tonight?"

"Of course. I couldn't leave you guys fight the bug all on your own."

"Thanks for your help."

The elevator pinged open.

"Do you fancy a drink?" she asked him as she pressed the button.

Zak had never noticed what a lovely smile she had.

"Just a quick nightcap to relax after all the stress," she added.

Just a minute ago, he had been desperate to go home but now he wasn't so keen anymore. "Sure," Zak replied.

She smiled again.

How come he had never noticed those beautiful eyes before?

***

The following day, Antonio and Carolina were sharing an ice cream sundae when a message pinged on both their phones. It was from the dating app.

"Due to a temporary fault in the system, you've been matched to the wrong person. We apologise for any inconvenience," the message read.

Antonio and Carolina chuckled, deleted the app and kissed.

9. NO MORE SECRETS

"What's so funny?" Melina asked Tanino. He was chuckling at his phone.

"It's nothing important. Just a joke from the boys."

Since Tanino and his friends had started a group chat, Tanino was often on his phone, smiling and chuckling.

"I want to laugh too," she said, feeling left out.

"It's just a silly in-joke," Tanino said dismissively. He dropped his phone into his pocket.

"By the way, has the doctor called back to give you an appointment?" Melina asked.

"Oh, yes, she has. Didn't I tell you?"

"No, you didn't. You must have told your friends," Melina said, miffed.

"I might have," Tanino said, missing the sarcasm in her tone.

"These days you tell them more than you tell me. But who will accompany you to the doctor—them or me?"

***

As soon as they got to the doctor's surgery, Tanino left Melina in the waiting room and rushed to the toilet.

It happened every time. The nerves of seeing the doctor must give Tanino a genuine physical urge to hide, Melina thought.

Tanino had left his phone on his chair and a message pinged. The screen showed that it was from someone called "Botcher".

Who could that be? The phone was unlocked. Intrigued, Melina picked it up and clicked on the message.

It contained a funny video of dancing cats. She chuckled. Someone called "Dogfather" immediately replied with an even funnier video of dancing dogs.

"What are you doing with my phone?"

Tanino's voice made Melina start and drop his phone back on the chair.

"You left it here and there were messages for you."

"Exactly. *For me.*" He sat down and checked the messages.

"Who are Botcher and Dogfather?" she asked.

"Just nicknames we give each other. You shouldn't be reading my messages." Tanino put his phone into his pocket.

"But you are my husband. There should be no secrets between husband and wife. Do you have a nickname too? What is it?"

"It doesn't matter," he answered tersely.

But it did matter to Melina. She couldn't bear the thought that Tanino was part of something she was excluded from. Just then, the doctor called them in.

"When did you start experiencing discomfort in this knee?" the doctor asked Tanino.

"About two years ago," Tanino replied.

"Less than that," Melina corrected. "You told me at Domenico's wedding, when I asked you to dance, remember?"

"I had been having pain a lot before that. I just hadn't told you," Tanino said.

Why hadn't he told her?

"Have you taken anything for it?" the doctor asked.

"Yes. I've used some anti-inflammatory cream," Tanino said.

Melina had had no idea. She hadn't seen him apply the cream and she didn't even know they had any. How many more things about her husband did she not know?

By the time they left the

doctor's room, Melina had made up her mind. She must learn everything about her husband.

***

Every morning around eleven o'clock, while Melina was in church or at the market, Tanino met up with his friends at Carmelo's café.

Over a cup of coffee and a custard croissant, they chatted and played cards. Since retiring from his job at the railway, Tanino had missed male company. These coffee mornings provided just that, and he treasured them.

That day, the boys were halfway through a game of *scopone*, with all the banter and laughter that came with it, when Tanino saw Melina step through the door.

His heart skipped a beat. Melina had never disturbed him there. There must be a serious problem. He jumped up.

"Is everything alright, dear?"

"Yes, of course. I've just come to join you for a bit," she said, pulling a chair from another table and sitting next to Tanino.

Silence fell over the scopone game, so that all you could hear was the humming of the ice cream fridges.

"Hello," she greeted everyone.

Tanino's friends, who were also the husbands of Melina's friends, greeted her back. The card game was resumed, minus the banter and the conversation.

Was Melina's madcap idea connected with her snooping in his phone at the doctor's surgery? He agreed that there shouldn't be secrets between them, but was there anything wrong in him having a space that was his own? Friends he didn't have to share with her? He shared everything else with her.

Melina broke the silence. "Which one of you is Botcher?"

The game stopped again, and everyone looked at Tanino, who felt like Judas. The unspoken rule of the group was that the content of their conversations wasn't for sharing outside the group.

"Melina saw a message coming up on my phone," he explained.

"I'm Botcher," one of the men admitted. "They call me that because I once botched a DIY job."

"Not only once—many

times!" Rocco put in.

Everyone laughed, including Melina, and the ice was broken.

Tanino was relieved to see that his friends weren't upset about his wife's intrusion. But he still felt uneasy. This was his personal space and Melina had broken in.

Back when he was working, she wouldn't have dreamed of joining him for his lunch break with his colleagues.

"Are you meeting again

tomorrow?" Melina asked him when they were walking home.

Was she intending to join him and his friends permanently? The prospect filled Tanino with panic. "No, we're not meeting tomorrow," he lied.

"How about the day after?"

"I don't think I'll go."

He wouldn't go back to Carmelo's café so long as there was a chance Melina would follow him there.

"What will you do instead?" she asked him.

"I think I'll stay at home."

"Then I'll stay too."

***

Melina sat with her knitting in her chair next to Tanino's one. Her project of learning anything about her husband that she didn't know had backfired.

Since she had started trying to penetrate the aspects of him she knew less well, he had recoiled away like a snail touched by a finger.

"What are you reading?" She peeked over the page of his magazine. He was doing a crossword. "'Submarine' can't be the answer. You need ten letters. Try 'underwater'," she suggested.

He struck through "submarine" and wrote "underwater." It fitted.

"For the vertical clue, try 'avowed'," she suggested now.

But Tanino's pen didn't

move.

"Aren't you going to try 'avowed'?" she persisted.

He put the magazine down. "Melina, if I wanted to know the answers, I would go to the last page. But perhaps I want to work them out myself, all on my own," he told her.

"Sorry." Melina resumed knitting.

This wasn't working. She had to find better ways to reach into the parts of his life he kept from her.

***

It was Wednesday afternoon—the day Melina and some of her friends cleaned the church.

This would distract her from her failures with Tanino. She enjoyed her friends' company and their camaraderie. She liked seeing the wooden pews shine and the marble floors glitter as a result of their work.

Melina got on with dusting the confessional booth. There were lots of nooks and crannies where dust could gather. She opened the red velvet curtain. Poor Father Pietro, it was such a small space! With a wooden bench and a wooden back, she couldn't imagine it being very comfortable to sit on for hours on end. Or was it? She had never tried.

Melina checked that none of her friends were looking and stepped inside. She sat down and closed the curtain. Yes, it felt a little claustrophobic.

Maybe it was better with the side window open. She slid the wooden shutter with a clunk and looked through the metal lattice. She had always wondered how much Father Pietro could see of her through it. Not much, it seemed.

A shadow fell over the metal lattice and the kneeler creaked. Oh, no—someone had come for confession! She wasn't supposed to be sitting there! Could she sneak out without being seen?

"Forgive me, Father, for I have sinned," a familiar voice said from the other side of the screen.

Melina froze. It was Tanino.

When she had set her mind on discovering everything about her husband, she hadn't meant in this way. This had to be her punishment for wanting to know more than he was willing to share.

Just then, steps approached on the church's stone floor.

"Father, what are you doing

there?" she heard Tanino ask.

"I could ask the same about you. There's no point in talking to an empty confessional," Father Pietro answered with a chuckle.

"I thought I heard someone inside," Tanino said.

A drop of cold sweat ran down Melina's back. She braced herself for the inevitable moment of her shame.

"It must have been the creaky old wood," Father

Pietro replied. "Come, let's go to my office where we can sit on comfortable chairs."

The kneeler creaked, Tanino's shadow disappeared from the window and Melina started breathing again.

She had learnt her lesson. She would not force her way into Tanino's private life ever again.

***

Since Melina had started reading his messages and turning up at his meetings with his friends, Tanino had kept his distance from her, and had felt guilty about it.

Father Pietro reassured him that protecting his private space wasn't a sin but had recommended that he be open with Melina about it.

When he got home, Tanino quickly noticed that Melina was avoiding him. For the past couple of weeks, she had hounded him like an eager puppy. Now that he needed only a few minutes of her time, she was slipping away like an eel.

"Can I have a word?" Tanino eventually asked.

Melina blanched. "I've got to start on supper."

"But we're in the kitchen. I just wanted to say that I'm sorry about being distant the past few days."

She looked relieved, as if she had expected him to say something else.

"It's fine. I shouldn't have

forced my way into your private spaces. Not everything has to be shared between husband and wife," she said.

Tanino had expected her to disagree. "What made you change your mind?" he asked, his arm around her shoulder.

Melina smiled. "I'm sorry, my love. I can't tell you. It's private."

10. A FRAGILE HEART

My mum and dad didn't live together. Mum and I lived on a little island called Pantelleria, and Dad lived in Sicily, which is also an island but so big that you can't see that it's got sea all around.

Every other weekend Dad came to pick me up and take me to his flat, and we did fun things like going to the mop fair to see all the shops. His flat was small, but he said it didn't matter because he was always at work.

My dad repairs people's hearts in the hospital. He's always very busy so people's hearts must get broken quite a lot.

One day, we were buying our hydrofoil tickets to go back to Pantelleria.

"One single and one return," Dad said. The return ticket was for him.

"I'm not sure that you can return today. There's a storm in the making," the ticketing man said.

"Let's stay here," I told Dad. I liked staying with him.

"I'm sorry, sweetheart, but I have an important conference tomorrow," Dad replied.

"I can stay in your flat while you go to the conference. I'll be good," I assured him.

Dad stroked my head and smiled. "Sorry, sweetie, not this time."

I was a bit sad because I wanted to stay longer with Dad, but at least I had the hydrofoil trip to look forward to. It's fun flying over the water.

But this time it wasn't fun at all. I felt so sick that Dad had to empty our bag of shopping.

"Due to the weather conditions, this is the last hydrofoil trip for today," the loudspeakers announced, and Dad ran a hand over his face and sighed.

"Does it mean that you're staying in Pantelleria?" I asked.

"No. I'll have to take a ferry or an aeroplane, but I'll be late home," he said, and I was disappointed.

When we got off the hydrofoil, Mum was waiting for me on the jetty. She gave a big smile to me but not to Dad.

"I've heard that this is the last hydrofoil for today. How are you getting back?" she asked him.

I thought that it was nice of Mum to worry about Dad.

"I'll try a ferry," he said.

"They're not running," she informed him.

Dad took a deep breath and looked at the empty taxi rank.

"I'll drive you to the airport," Mum said, which was nice of her.

Mum drove to the airport very fast, and Dad leapt out of the car and ran into the building faster than I'd ever seen him run before.

"I didn't get to say goodbye," I protested.

Looking at the clouds chasing each other in the sky, Mum smiled. "Don't worry. I don't think he's going anywhere."

But she said it as if it wasn't a good thing.

"Is that why we are waiting here instead of going home?"

"Yes. I want to be sure that he's gone."

Mum was right and Dad came back.

"All flights are cancelled! I'll miss my conference!" he exclaimed, waving his arms like an angry puppet.

"You need to get yourself a room before all the hotels are full," Mum told him.

"Can't Dad stay with us?"

Neither of them heard me, because they continued talking.

"I've already tried. Everywhere is full," Dad said.

Mum let out a long breath. "What about your sister?"

"I don't want to cause tension between her and her husband."

"This is the first time you've worried about breaking up a family," Mum snapped.

Dad looked at his feet. "Do you have any friends who could put me up?"

"Can't Dad stay with us?" I asked again, louder this time.

"Not after what I've told them about you, they won't," Mum replied to him, ignoring me.

"Why can't Dad stay with us?" I shouted.

Finally they were quiet.

Mum sighed again. "This is precisely what I wanted to avoid. No way."

"How about Dad pays us like we were a hotel?" I suggested.

Mum often told me that if we had more money we could do this and that, so I was sure that she would like to be paid like a hotel.

Mum tapped her chin. "All right. But I don't want money. Your father will make it up to us another way. Are you coming, Pietro?"

Dad nodded and got into the car. He didn't look like he

wanted it very much, but I think that he had no choice.

When we got home, Mum showed him all the things that were broken, like the blinds in my bedroom, the boiler and the kitchen cabinet with the wonky door.

Dad smiled, got the toolbox out of the cupboard and began to work.

***

The next morning, I found Dad asleep on the sofa. He was

wearing the same clothes as the day before.

"Dad, would you like to borrow some pyjamas?"

He opened one eye. "Thank you, but I don't think they'd fit me. But you can give me a new toothbrush if you know where they are."

"I'll ask Mum where she keeps them."

He caught my arm. "No, don't. It's okay. I can do without."

"Why are you sleeping here? Mum's bed is big and she lets me sleep there when I've had a bad dream."

"I'm very comfy here," he said, straightening his neck with a cracking sound.

We went to the kitchen to have breakfast while Mum was still sleeping. When we washed up after our breakfast, he sighed.

"This sink is blocked," he declared.

He found the stick with the brown rubber cup and pushed it up and down over the plug of the sink, making sounds that made me laugh. We both laughed when yucky black gunk sprayed out of the overflow hole and straight on to his shirt.

Mum didn't laugh or smile now that Dad was staying with us, though, even if he was doing lots of good things for her.

When everything in the house was fixed, Dad began shopping and cooking, and Mum was surprised when she got home from work and found the table laid and the food all ready. I saw that she wanted to smile but stopped herself.

"Why can't you stay with us forever?" I asked Dad at dinnertime.

"My job is in Trapani."

"There's a hospital here too. Can you ask them if they'll take you?"

But before Dad answered, Mum told me to eat up my pasta, and Dad didn't answer. After dinner, Mum and I went to visit Grandma and Auntie.

"Is it true, Nunzia, that you've taken Pietro back?" Grandma asked as soon as we sat down in the kitchen.

"No. I'm just putting him up until the storm is over. He has nowhere to stay."

"Good. Be careful not to fall for him again after what he's done," Auntie said.

I wanted to ask what he'd done, but Grandma said, "Not in front of the child", so I never found out.

"Is he still living in sin?" Grandma asked Mum.

"No. He lives in Trapani," I answered.

The three of them smiled.

"I think so." Mum nodded.

"Is Sin in Trapani?" I asked, but Grandma began talking about the storm.

I was worried for Dad because I didn't know where Sin was and it sounded like it wasn't a good place.

So that night, when Mum had gone to bed and Dad was getting comfortable on the sofa, I went to see him.

"You should be in bed," Dad told me.

"I can't sleep," I explained. "Mum thinks that you are living in Sin, Dad. Where's that?"

He sighed. "I made a mistake once for a very short time. My sin lasted only a week."

Now that I was reassured, I went to bed and fell asleep.

***

I burst into Mum's room at seven o'clock, because that was the time when I was allowed to wake her up.

"Dad doesn't live in Sin anymore! He told me last night that he only went there for one week!"

Mum's eyelids flew open like the eyes of a doll when you tip it up quickly.

"What?"

"Dad doesn't live in Sin anymore. He was there only for one week," I repeated.

Her cheeks went red. "Did you ask him?"

"Yes."

Mum rolled her eyes and covered her face with the blanket.

That day Mum put my favourite film on TV and stayed in the kitchen with Dad for a long time with the door closed.

They had red eyes when they came out, but they didn't look angry. They hugged me a lot.

The next day, Mum wore her beautiful pink dress to go to work and, when she got home, Dad had cooked pasta with mussels and opened a bottle of wine. They drank it and Mum giggled a lot. Because she looked so happy, when she put me to bed I was brave.

"What did Dad do to you when I was little?"

She stared at her hands. "He broke my heart."

"I'm sure he didn't do it on purpose. His job is fixing hearts," I told her.

"Yes. Maybe it was a mistake."

***

The wind stopped, the sea calmed down and Dad booked his flight to go back to Trapani.

"I don't want you to leave," I sobbed.

"I'll be back, don't worry," he said, winking.

He was in a good mood, but I wanted him to be as sad as me. He didn't have a suitcase, so I took one of our shopping bags and I filled it with things for him. Flowers from the garden, a pebble, the drawings

I had made for him, and his toothbrush.

He looked into the bag and smiled. "Thank you, but I think I'll leave this toothbrush here."

I felt good because that meant he was coming back.

But when I got up in the morning, Dad wasn't on the sofa. My heart felt like a scrunched-up piece of paper and my throat became painful and tight. I burst into Mum's room.

"Dad has left without saying goodbye!" I shouted.

Mum's head whipped to the other side of the bed and guess who was there?

Their faces turned red. "I'm here. I had a bad dream," Dad explained.

I climbed into bed with them and hugged him. I was very happy that he hadn't left us without saying goodbye, and because Mum must have forgiven him.

When we got to the airport, Mum and Dad went behind a column where they thought I couldn't see them, and they kissed.

"Am I still going to stay with Dad next weekend?" I asked Mum when we were driving home.

"No, my love."

"Oh, please, Mum!"

"I'm sorry, you can't. Because he's coming here."

That was okay by me!

After that, Dad came every weekend and, each time, he left something behind. Mum gave him a drawer in her cupboard to keep his clothes in.

One day, he came by ferry. His car was so full of things that the back seats were squashed down.

"I have a job in the hospital here. I'm not going away anymore," he told me.

Now one half of Mum's cupboard belongs to Dad. He

still goes away when he has a conference, but he always comes back to us.

Sometimes people stop Mum in the street and ask her if she's taken my dad back, and she says yes. Some of them give her good wishes, but others shake their heads. Mum just smiles and walks on.

You don't have to care what other people say when your heart has been fixed.

The End

Other books by Stefania Hartley

Collections of short stories:

Sand, Sea & Tamburello

Stars Are Silver

Welcome to Quayside

Drive Me Crazy

Fresh from the Sea

A Slip of the Tongue

What's Yours is Mine

A Season of Goodwill

Tales from the Parish

Romance novellas:

The Italian Fake Date

Sweet Competition for Camillo's Café

Second Chances at Mamma's Trattoria

Under Far Eastern Skies

Cosy mysteries:

Father Roberto and the Missing Money

ABOUT THE AUTHOR

Stefania was born in Sicily and immediately started growing, but not very much. She left her sunny island after falling head over heels in love with an Englishman and now she lives in the UK with her husband and their three children. Having finally learnt English, she's enjoying it so much that she now writes short stories and novels. She'd love you to leave a review and to sign up for her newsletter at: www.stefaniahartley.com/sub scribe

so she can let you know when a new book is out. You'll also receive an exclusive short story.

Printed in Great Britain
by Amazon

54342411R00126